To my Nana Rosetta, the trailblazer, and to my parents, for building my confidence with each move.
–C.K.

To Gill, Jaira, Gerald, and my family, for believing in me.
–C.G.

978-1-953859-07-5 (Hardcover)
978-1-953859-05-1 (Paperback)
978-1-953859-06-8 (E-Book)

Library of Congress Control Number: 2021900908

Text by Ceece Kelley
Illustrations by Chloe Guevara
Book design by Tobi Carter
Edited by Nadara "Nay" Merrill

First edition 2021.

Soaring Kite Books
Washington, D.C.
United States of America
www.soaringkitebooks.com

Georgie Dupree
Drawn to Friends

Story by
Ceece Kelley

Pictures by
Chloe Guevara

Soaring Kite Books

"This is the worst day of my whole life!"

Georgie Dupree fidgets in her seat between "The Js"—her twin brothers Julian and James.

Georgie and her family are moving from Louisiana to Washington, D.C. to be with her Nana.

Georgie wonders if she will ever have any friends again.

Georgie already misses Bea, who was her best friend and next-door neighbor. They have matching necklaces to remember each other by while they are apart.

The Js never have to worry about leaving their best friend.

They are always together.

The Js play and giggle during the whole ride,
but Georgie is unusually quiet.

She doesn't belt out her
favorite songs,

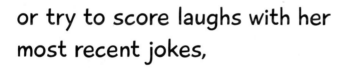

or try to score laughs with her
most recent jokes,

or even try to impress her
family with her latest drawings.

But when the family pulls into the city, Georgie perks right up...

"Goodness gracious! This place is BIG, Mama!

Look at all of these people! And all of these fancy buildings!"

"See, Georgie! You pouted for weeks for nothing. Isn't it beautiful?" Mama asks.

Georgie isn't going to let Mama win so easily.

"All right, everybody out!"

Daddy exhales with a laugh.

Georgie chews her bottom lip.

Nana's is the bright yellow house covered in ivy.
Now, Georgie lives in the bright yellow house covered in ivy too.

Georgie makes a beeline toward Nana.

She hugs and kisses Nana so quickly that she nearly knocks her over.

"My, my, my! Look at you, sugar!" Nana says, catching her balance. But Georgie is already off to get a closer look at the house.

Georgie's heart sinks. This living room doesn't have all the memories that her old one had. It hasn't hosted family charades, or karaoke with Bea, or sleepovers with all her friends laughing late into the night.

There is only one thing familiar about this living room—the smell of last night's fried dinner **swirling in the air** around her.

Georgie races up the old, creaky stairs to look for her room. The last room at the end of the hall has a big sparkly "G" on the door just for her, but it doesn't have...

a painted flower mural,
or a window that looks toward Bea's house, or
even a closet big enough for a reading fort.

It simply isn't home.

Georgie plops down the stairs one by one
and finds Mama in the living room.

"Mama, I miss my old room.
This new one just won't do!"

"Mind your manners, Georgie,"
Mama says in a hushed tone.

"I'm sure you can find a way to make it your own. Go on... get your things."

Mama kisses Georgie firmly on the forehead and sends her on her way.

Georgie drags her feet
on her way outside.

But then she sees a neighbor
and instantly trades her pouty
lip for a big smile.

"Hi, ma'am! I'm
Georgie Dupree, and
I just moved here all the way
from Louisiana. Do you
have any kids who want
to be my friends?"

"Well, hi there, Georgie!"

the neighbor says, surprised by Georgie's burst of energy.

"There are kids right next door, but they are in high school..."

"But I can play with big kids!"
she says to herself. "Everyone thinks I'm fun!"
Georgie smooths her outfit, takes a deep breath,
and knocks on the door of the older kids' house.

Waiting, waiting... nothing. Drats!
No one is home.

She drags her feet once more as she
walks back toward the house.

"Georgie, what is the matter now?"

"I don't have anyone to be my friend.
At home, I had my best friend, Bea, next door
and other kids my age in the neighborhood too!"

"Keep your chin up, Georgie.
Give it some time, sugar.
Don't forget that your family is always here for you."

"Right!" Georgie says with a snap of her finger.
"I can play with all of you for now!"

"I'm sorry, sugar, I can't play hopscotch right now. I've gotta get dinner on the table. It's your first night here, and I want to make it extra special. We're having my famous gumbo and king cake!"

Georgie left the kitchen holding back tears.

"I WANT TO GO BACK HOME!"

"I'm going to the car and
I'm not coming back inside!
I'll bet I can live at Bea's house.
Please take me back home!"

Daddy catches Georgie on her way outside
and sits her down on the front steps.

"Daddy, I'm sorry for yelling at everybody.

But my room isn't the same, there are no kids here my
age, and all of you are too busy to play with me!

It's just not home."

"Today was a tough day for everyone. But Nana is whippin' up your favorite dish for dinner! Just give it a chance. And don't forget,

I have a big day planned for us tomorrow!"

Georgie pouts through dinner...

and up until bedtime.

The next day, Georgie wakes up feeling hopeful because Daddy promised her a great day today.

And she had loved seeing all of the people and all of the fancy buildings downtown, after all.

Georgie rushes down
the stairs for breakfast,
eats quickly, then urges her family to
"get a move on" as Daddy would say.

Then she hurries
everyone out of the house
and to the bus stop at the
top of their street.

Georgie steps off the bus and is filled with the vibration of the music from the street performers, the doughy smell from the pretzel vendor, and the rush of people whooshing past her. Then Georgie sees an artsy lady making a big drawing on the ground.

"Excuse me, ma'am, what are you doing, and can I play?"

"It's chalk art," the artsy lady says smoothly. "I'm a chalk artist, and I draw large artwork on the street for people to enjoy. Then people like you come and talk to me about it! Here, you try."

"Come along now, Georgie," Nana says. "There's much more to see this way!"

Georgie's heart beats faster and faster as the wheels start to turn in her head.

She loves to draw in her sketchbook.

She loves to play with chalk for hopscotch.

But she never thought of trying them together to make large artwork for everyone to see.

"If I make my masterpiece by Nana's house,
maybe people will come play with me too!
Maybe then I can make some friends!"

Georgie skips through the streets for the rest of the day
while she thinks about her fool-proof plan.

Back at home, Georgie is still buzzing about
her new plan. She lays out all of her chalk
colors and lets her creativity flow.

She has so much fun playing by
herself that for just a minute,

she forgets she doesn't
have any friends.

"Excuse me, what are you doing, and can we play?" a boy asks.

"It's chalk art," Georgie says smoothly. "I'm a chalk artist, and I draw large artwork on the street for people to enjoy. Then kids like you come and talk to me about it."

"That's awesome! I'm Camila and this is Quinn. I've lived in this neighborhood my whole life and I've never seen you before."

"I'm Georgie Dupree, and I just moved here all the way from Louisiana. I live with my Nana in that bright yellow house covered in ivy!"

Georgie is so excited that for just a minute,
she forgets to miss home.

Georgie Dupree Series

DON'T MISS THESE OTHER GEORGIE DUPREE BOOKS!

Classroom Confidence: I'm starting at a new school and I can't wait for you to see how I overcome my first day jitters.

Sharing the Stage: I've just got to get the lead in the school play! But if I don't, can I still find a way to shine on stage?

Parents & Teachers

THE FUN DOESN'T STOP HERE!

You can find literacy and social studies
lesson plans for teachers along
with a classroom mural art activity
at georgiedupree.com.